PRESENTED TO

Pat

_____

Love, FROM

"Mary Ever"

_____

DATE

Jan 2002

_____

SEARCHING FOR THE

SONG

SEARCHING FOR THE

SONG

by Mary Ann

illustrated by Harry

Dedicated to

The angels in our lives

who have touched

our hearts

and

made them sing

ABOUT THE BOOK

This is partly the story of little Zachariah. He travels around the world trying to help people discover the music within their own hearts, and then sing along with him and his companions.

In a way, there's another part of the story that only you can tell.

They're restless in the countryside,

The city troops are bleak,

And forces in the hills complain

There's barely time to sleep.

The scouts who tend the watch at sea

Are sick of lonely tours,

And those who guard the coastline

Want more help along the shores.

The job seems hardly worth it

And respect is ebbing low,

If something isn't done, and soon,

Defensive lines may go.

Michael felt discouraged as
he

Put down Gabe's report,

With rumor there might be a
strike

They could wind up in Court.

"Get me Gabriel", he boomed,

"Make that A-S-A-P";

His order crackled through
the Net

To every company.

10

Within a nanosecond Gabe

Was standing in the room;

He saw the lines on Michael's
brow

And felt a sense of doom.

"What's going on here",
Michael asked,

"When this gets to The
Boss,

I fear that what may
happen

Will be every spirit's
loss."

"Well, Michael, things
are not the same

And doubt is setting in;

There's more to do for
angels now

Than dancing on a pin."

"Faith and hope are hard to find,

And love is scarcer yet;

Just when we think they've seen the light,

They all seem to forget."

18

As Gabe went on the angel
chiefs

Joined in with the debate,

And gave their views of
what was wrong

Outside the Pearly Gate.

Zachariah Angel edged

His way into the crowd;

In awe of all the big
wings

There was no retreating
now.

"Excuse me, please. I had
a thought

That might be worth a try;

I'd like to run it past you

Just to see if it can fly."

Raphael let out a sigh

And Gabriel looked away,

But Michael coaxed the
cherub on

To hear what he would say.

"Well, Sir", said Zachariah then,

"We can't do it alone,

It's getting harder all the time

To lead the people Home."

"What if we joined up
forces

So they'd help us in our
task;

Not all of them might get
the drift

But surely we could ask."

"Ridiculous, below us",
said

A big wing to his side;

"Careful", Michael warned
them all,

"You know what comes with
pride."

Then Zachariah trembled
but

He wasn't giving in;

He had this chance to let
them see

What victories they could
win.

"I stopped to sing a song
of praise

On top of Hong Kong's Peak,

And met a Buddhist
Millionaire

Whose faith was growing
weak."

"We looked out on the
valley and

I slowly turned his gaze

To where the peasants
lived and worked

In such unhappy ways."

"It wasn't long before he thought

Of things that he could do

To make their lives much easier

And boost his business too."

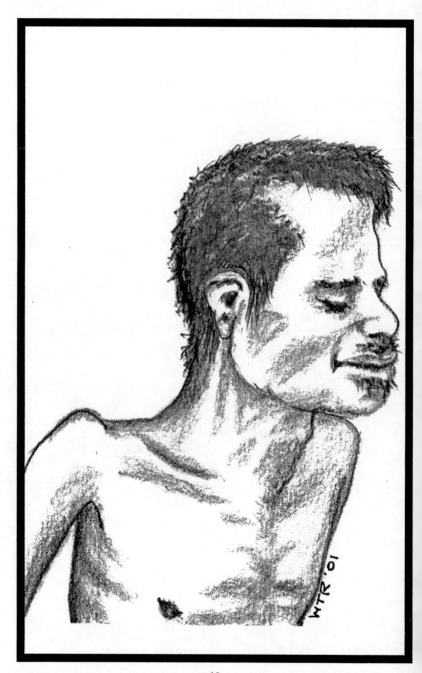

"And when I reached Calcutta

In the middle of the night,

The roads were filled with
homeless,

It was such a painful sight."

"I found a Hindu princess
there

With kind and loving heart,

Just waiting for encourage-
ment

That she could have a part

WTR '01

44

"In bringing hope for better
times

To people on the street;

She opened up her palace
doors

And gave them food to eat."

WTR '01

46

"As I approached Jerusalem

The sky was all aglow,

With light surrounding
Church and Mosque

And Temple Wall below."

48

"The sound of song and
worship rose

Above the City wall;

The peace they wanted in
their hearts

Was meant for one and all."

"Above the lands of Africa

The clouds were very dark,

Destruction from the tragic
wars

Had left its deadly mark."

WTR '01

52

"I flapped my wings repeatedly

And caused the ground to
shake,

As soldiers from opposing
sides

Took shelter from the quake."

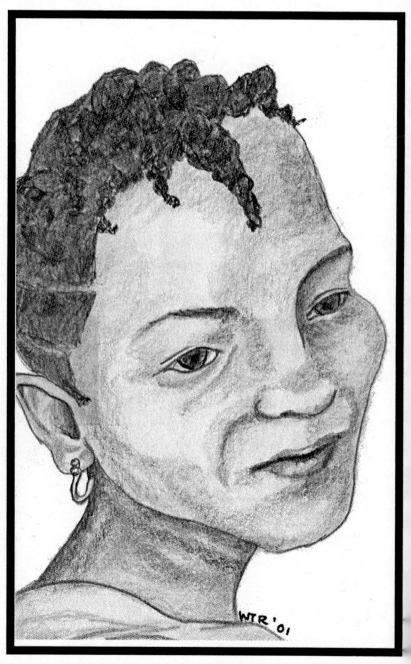

Seeking safety in the fields,

Afraid of being killed,

The longtime foes found hopes
of peace

Remained within them still."

"And then I passed by Wall Street

In the middle of the day;

You know how people rush about

In such a frantic way."

"A CEO in three-piece suit

Was outside Federal Hall

With nothing on his mind
except

The Nasdaq rise and fall."

"I told him that the chips
were down

And that the greatest shares

Of dividends were waiting

For someone who really cares."

"He went back to the office,

Gave a bonus to his staff,

Set up a trust for needy
kids

And took some time to laugh."

"As I've been checking out
the way

That things are getting done,

From Rio to Nairobi and

From Perth to Washington,

"From Moscow to Islamabad,

From Cork to Molikai,

Each person that I spoke to

Had an empty place inside."

"It seems for some strange reason

Many people tend to think

The only time to look for us

Is when they're on the brink."

70

"Now, I don't know exactly how

Love travels on its way,

But little joys seem cast aside

In every busy day:

"Dew drops on the flowers
and

A bird's song in the park,

The murmuring of ocean tides

And stars that light the
dark;

"The comfort of a friendly
smile,

And children having fun;

If we rejoice in little
things

Then when temptations come

"We may find ourselves
inspired

To do the things we should,

And won't keep harping on
what's bad,

But focus on what's good."

"Nothing big, Sir, that I
know,

Just simple notes to play

Within the concert of the soul

For people on their way."

"If those on earth could sing
with us

Some little words of praise

In hidden moments of their
lives,

There could be brighter days

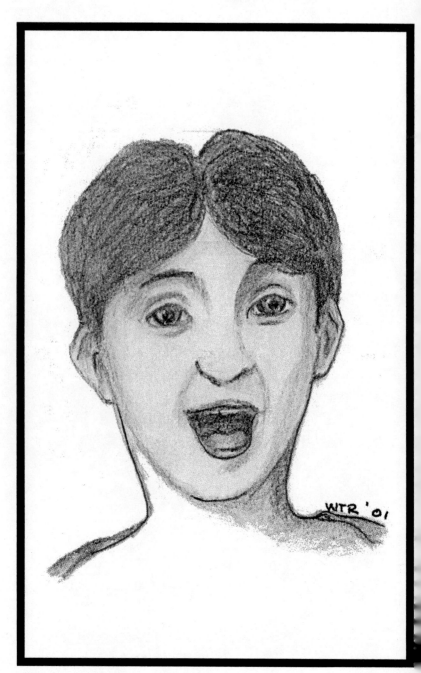

"For men and women, angels too,

No matter what we do;

And when we're tempted to give up

The song could see us through."

84

"I'm sure The Boss has thought of this,

He thinks of everything",

Said Michael as he opened wide

The power of his wings.

"I'll check it out this
instant though

And see what I can do;

I know The Boss takes old
ideas

And turns them into new."

When Michael came back to the spot

Where Zachariah stood,

He said, "The Boss has answered

In the way I thought He would;

"He told me I should 'keep
the faith',

And as I turned to leave

He said the song is in us
all

If we would just believe."

"Tell me, Michael, what He means",

And letting out a sigh,

Little Zachariah looked

As though he'd start to cry.

"It's mystery to me, as well,

Just like it always was;

We might not have the
answers, but

The Boss, He surely does."

"We'll sing the song we've always sung,

The ageless, joyful song;

Not everyone may know the words,

But they can hum along."

"Thank you, little cherub",
Michael

Beamed a friendly smile;

"Your thoughts were locked
inside our own

And waited there a while

"Until the time was right
once more

To brighten up the earth

With strains of happy music
and

The lilting sound of mirth."

The news went through the
Heavens then,

Upon the land and sea,

From East to West, from pole
to pole

Where human hearts may be;

And Michael gave instructions
to

The angels for their course:

"We're singing with the
folks below

On orders from The Boss!"

The street was very quiet as

A bell began to peale;

I wondered, was I dreaming
this

Or could it be for real?

AUTHOR, "Mary Ann", is a mother and grandmother who has been writing stories, poetry and essays for many years. Her children's story, "The Land of Light", written under penname, was recently published by 1st Books Library, and a few of her poems appear in the Staten Island Poetry Society Anthology for the year 2000.

ILLUSTRATOR, "Harry", is a poet and art teacher in a Staten Island, New York high school where he oversees the creative aspects of the year-book. For the past five years, he has designed and taught an evening arts enrichment program, featuring painting, sculpture, music and literature from various periods, the most recent being Twentieth Century Arts.

Printed in the United States
2503